'...
Shelby attacked on ...
wing.

Jordan, the left-back, missed his tackle and
...tthew had plenty of time and space to pick
...a target for his centre. He dallied too long,
...lt for choice, and Jordan recovered well
...gh to have a second bite.

...er Matthew went, toppling to the ground
... a chopped-down tree. The referee
...istled immediately and pointed to the
...nalty spot.

... won the ball,' cried Jordan. 'I never even
...uched him.'

...ul challenge from behind,' said the referee
...rnly. 'No arguing . . .'

# ROB CHILDS

# THE BIG FIX

## YOUNG CORGI BOOKS

THE BIG FIX
A YOUNG CORGI BOOK : 0 552 454341

First publication in Great Britain

PRINTING HISTORY
Young Corgi edition published 1998

Copyright © 1998 by Rob Childs
Illustrations copyright © 1998 by Aidan Potts

Set in 14/18pt Linotype New Century Schoolbook by
Phoenix Typesetting, Ilkley, West Yorkshire.

Young Corgi Books are published by Transworld Publishers Ltd,
61–63 Uxbridge Road, Ealing, London W5 5SA,
in Australia by Transworld Publishers (Australia) Pty. Ltd,
15–25 Helles Avenue, Moorebank, NSW 2170,
and in New Zealand by Transworld Publishers (NZ) Ltd,
3 William Pickering Drive, Albany, Auckland.

Printed in Great Britain by Clays Ltd, St Ives plc

*Especially for all referees!*

# 1 Referee!

'Offside, ref!'

The goalkeeper's loud appeal was ignored. So, too, were the claims from the other Danebridge defenders. Their arms were raised in vain.

'Play on!' bellowed the referee.

They had no choice. Nor did they have any hope of catching the Shenby winger. Matthew cut inside for goal, looking to increase his team's lead. Only the keeper barred his way.

But that keeper was Chris Weston,

the Danebridge captain, who also wore the number 1 jersey for the Area side. Chris raced off his line, forcing Matthew to make a hasty decision. To shoot or to dribble.

He shot. He tried to place the ball wide of the onrushing keeper, but Chris's speedy advance narrowed the gap too quickly. The save was top class, straight out of the coaching manual. Chris stayed on his feet until the last moment, then spread his body and blocked the shot with his outstretched leg. The ball cannoned away to safety.

'Great stop!' cried Philip, the Danebridge centre-back. 'They didn't deserve to score. He was miles offside.'

Philip didn't care if his remarks got him into trouble with the referee. He was still cross about Shenby's first 'goal'. The winger had clearly controlled the ball with his hand before shooting.

The home school's referee, their sports teacher, had turned a blind eye to the offence. What made it even harder to take was the brief exchange of words overheard between the referee and the scorer.

'Good goal, Matt, well taken.'

'Thanks, Dad.'

The result of this match meant more than usual to the players involved. Not only was it a local derby between the primary schools of neighbouring villages, but it was also a second round cup-tie.

Danebridge had spent most of the game so far pressed back on defence, but Chris knew there wasn't long to go now until half-time.

'Just hope we can hold out,' he muttered under his breath. 'It's no

thanks to this ref we're only losing one–nil.'

The main thanks, in fact, were due to the captain himself. Even before Shenby had scored their controversial goal, Chris had twice frustrated them with superb saves. A point-blank header had been tipped over the crossbar, and this was followed by a spectacular catch from a deflected shot.

'Here they come again,' Chris groaned as Shenby attacked once more up the right wing.

Jordan, the left-back, missed his tackle and Matthew had plenty of time and space to pick out a target for his centre. He dallied too long, spoilt for

choice, and Jordan recovered well to have a second bite.

Over Matthew went, toppling to the ground like a chopped-down tree. The referee whistled immediately and pointed to the penalty spot.

'I won the ball,' cried Jordan. 'I never even touched him.'

'Foul challenge from behind,' said the referee sternly. 'No arguing.'

Matthew smirked at the goalkeeper

as he placed the ball on the spot, but Chris didn't respond. He was totally focused on the job in hand – trying to keep the ball out of his net.

'OK, son, when you're ready,' said his father.

Matthew ran in and blasted the ball, relying solely on power to do the trick. It worked. Chris dived to his left, but the ball went dead straight – right where he'd been standing.

He lay on the ground, cursing his luck. 'If I'd stayed where I was, I'd have swallowed it.'

Chris's grandad was watching, dismayed, from the touchline. He was the school team's biggest fan and rarely missed a game, home or away.

'This is one of the worst examples of biased refereeing I've ever seen,' he said to Mr Jones, Danebridge's headmaster. 'This chap's far too keen for his own side to win. Who is he?'

The headmaster sighed. 'A new teacher of theirs called Mr Walters. He only started here this term.'

Chris led the complaints as his teammates gathered together at half-time. 'The ref ought to be wearing a blue shirt like his son.'

'Yeah, that kid of his took a dive,' insisted Jordan.

'Bet they practise diving in drama

lessons here,' Philip sneered.

Mr Jones was annoyed himself at some of the referee's decisions, but tried hard not to let it show to the players.

'I know it can be difficult at times, lads,' he said sympathetically, 'but remember that old saying in football: the referee is always right – even when he's wrong.'

# 2 Cut Short

Danebridge and Shenby had both made a promising start to the season. The two schools were riding high in the league table and also looking forward to a good cup run. One of them, however, was in for a disappointment.

Midway through the second half, the visitors' chances of being in the next round appeared slim. Danebridge were still trailing 2–0 to a team that could do no wrong in the eyes of the referee.

Fouls by Shenby continued to go unpunished and free-kicks were awarded in their favour at every opportunity. Often the players had no idea why they had been penalized.

'I don't believe this guy!' Philip muttered as Mr Walters gave another corner instead of a goal-kick after the ball came off a Shenby knee.

'Good job Pud's not here,' said Jordan. 'He'd be going ballistic!'

Mr Jones, too, was relieved about the absence of their usual number nine. He guessed Pud's short temper would have blown a fuse by now and made matters far worse. Danebridge might have been reduced to ten men.

'Mark up tight, defence,' shouted Chris as Matthew prepared to take the corner. 'Get to the ball first.'

Philip made sure he did just that. His height was a great advantage at set-pieces. He rose well above friend and foe alike to head the ball firmly away out of danger. It dropped at the feet of Jamie Robertson, Danebridge's wizard of the dribble.

Freckle-faced Jamie may have been the baby of the team in terms of age, but he was their most skilful player. The little winger had had very few touches of the ball up to this moment and now meant to keep it to himself. There was nothing he enjoyed more than a long solo dribble.

Jamie scampered off along the touchline, drawing opponents towards him like moths to a flame. They closed in, one behind the other for extra

cover, as if queuing up to be mesmerized by his dazzling footwork.

'He's up to his tricks again,' laughed Jordan. 'We might as well all have a sit down for a bit till he gets tired.'

Jamie pranced and danced his way past most of the bewildered defenders, but in the end, he overdid it – as usual. Trying one trick too many, he beat himself rather than had the ball taken off him. It bobbled loose in the penalty area and was hastily hacked away.

Not very far. The miskicked clearance went to the only Danebridge player who had followed up Jamie's run. Ryan was lurking on the edge of the area, just inside the 'D'. He took one touch to control the ball and then one more to drive it low past the keeper into the net.

There was no doubt that Pud's strength and power had been missed in attack, but not even he could have hit the shot any better than Ryan. Nor could the referee find an excuse to disallow such a well-struck goal.

'That was sloppy defending,' cried Mr Walters. 'Wake up!'

Shenby were jolted into action as if their alarm clock had just gone off. They bombarded Chris's goal with shots and crosses, and Danebridge could barely get the ball out of their own half. Something had to give.

No-one could complain about Shenby's third goal. Dominic, their captain, deserved the credit for it, bursting through a gap into a good scoring position himself. He feinted to shoot, wrong-footing Chris, then unselfishly switched the ball to the unmarked Matthew. The winger only had to tap it over the line to complete his hat-trick.

At 3–1, the cup-tie seemed to be settled, but Mr Jones knew that his team would never give up. He glanced at his watch – and so did Grandad.

'Still got time,' Grandad called out. 'C'mon, you can do it, Reds.'

Shenby were caught dozing again. They had relaxed their guard after scoring and paid the price. The red and white striped shirts of Danebridge sliced through their casual defence and Jamie dribbled round the goal-keeper to finish off the move in style.

'Oh dear, they'll be for it on Monday morning,' chuckled Grandad, seeing the referee's furious expression. 'Let's hope for their sakes that he cools down over the weekend.'

Mr Jones studied his watch again. 'A couple of minutes left at least,' he said. 'We might snatch a replay yet.'

But as Danebridge regained possession from the restart and Ryan sprinted forward with the ball, a long, shrill blast rent the air.

'Full-time!' the referee called out. 'Shenby win 3–2.'

'Never! He's gone and blown early,' exclaimed Grandad. 'What a rotten thing to do!'

The substitutes nearby heard Grandad's remark and were quick to tell their teammates what had

happened. They felt cheated. Chris always made a point, as captain, of shaking the referee's hand after the match, but not on this occasion. He deliberately snubbed him.

Dominic came to slump next to Chris as he removed his muddy boots outside the cloakroom. 'Soz about the ref. I know how you must be feeling,' he began. 'We're fed up with him too. He spoils our games.'

'Really?' grunted Chris, standing up.

'So what are you going to do about it? I didn't hear any of you objecting when he gave that penalty.'

\*

On the way home, Chris, Philip and Jordan sat together in the back of Grandad's car. It was a quiet journey. The full shock of Danebridge's early exit from the cup was taking some time to sink in.

'Can't wait till we meet them in the league,' said Jordan as they stopped by his house. 'It'll be a real grudge match.'

'Yeah, revenge is sweet!' muttered Philip.

'Just hope it's at home so we don't have to suffer their ref again,' Chris said, and saw Grandad frown.

'I'm afraid not, m'boy. Mr Jones told me we're due back at their place in a fortnight's time!'

Grandad dropped Philip off too before he spoke his mind to Chris. 'I reckon it might not be a bad idea for Mr Jones to postpone that league game. Y'know, give things a bit longer to blow over.'

Chris pulled a face. 'It'd look as if we're wimps or something, too scared to play them.'

Grandad sighed. 'Well, if it does go ahead, it'll be up to you to lead by example.'

'How do you mean?'

'It's always important to play the game in the right spirit, no matter what, and you must spell that out to your team. They'll listen to you – even hotheads like that Pud. You've got their respect.'

'But it made me so mad as well today.'

'Aye, maybe, but you can't play football properly if you lose your temper. Cool heads, that's what it's going to take to outwit that ref and beat his team fair and square.'

# 3 Gunpowder Plot

It wasn't only Pud who perhaps lacked a cool head, especially on Bonfire Night. Philip and Jordan were standing rather too close to the heat of the roaring bonfire on the village recreation ground.

They were both still grumbling about the Shenby defeat.

'Reckon it was all a big fix from the start,' Jordan sneered.

Philip nodded as he munched on a hot dog. 'Yeah, now we know why

games are sometimes called *fixtures*!'

They watched a rocket whoosh up into the dark sky and explode in a brief, bright flare of coloured lights.

'Right, but somehow we'll have to make sure that ref doesn't get away with it again in the league match,' said Jordan.

Mustard dribbled down Philip's chin and he wiped it off with the sleeve of his jacket. 'Well, Pud will be back in the team then,' he spluttered. 'He won't stand for any sort of nonsense.'

Jordan pointed Pud out near the hot-dog stand. 'Look, he's over there, stuffing himself silly as usual. He's got food in both paws.'

'Said he was off school with an upset stomach,' Philip grinned. 'Not surprised. If I were his stomach, I'd be upset too!'

'Look who's talking, the amount of

31

grub you've put away this evening.'

'I'm a growing lad.'

'It's about time you stopped. If you grow any taller, you'll be more use at netball than football.'

'Don't you mean basketball?'

'No, netball. If the girls fastened a net round your head, they could use you as a post for shooting practice!'

Another cascade of lights burst over the crowd enjoying the firework display. But what made Chris suddenly jump was the thump of a heavy hand on his shoulder. He hadn't seen Andrew sneak up on him from behind.

'Bet I know who you'd like to see

on top of that bonfire instead of poor old Guy Fawkes, eh, little brother?' Andrew sniggered.

A number of people, including Andrew, sprang instantly to mind. Chris hated being called little brother. Although he was two years younger, he was rapidly catching up in height.

'Wally!' Andrew cackled. 'That's what the Shenby lot call that Walters bloke you've been droning on about all week.'

'How do you know that?'

''Cos my pal here told me. Gaz, come and meet my little brother.'

The youth strolled across to them, a can of cola in his hand. He took a long swig as he sized Chris up.

'So you're this keeper that my own kid brother reckons stopped them scoring double figures?'

'Come off it,' Chris snorted. 'It wasn't

that one-sided. Shenby were hanging
on at the end, despite all the ref's
cheating. Who is your brother,
anyway?'

'Dominic,' he smirked.

Chris turned on Andrew. 'You didn't
tell me you knew their captain's
brother.'

'You never asked. Gaz is a good mate
of mine at school. We're both gonna
come and watch your league match at

Shenby. We want to see this Wally in action.'

Chris groaned. 'There's probably going to be enough bother as it is. You two won't exactly help the situation.'

'Ah, but that's where you're wrong, our kid,' Andrew began before being interrupted by a series of deafening bangs. 'If things go to plan, it sounds like you can expect a few fireworks that day as well . . .'

*

'Now we're out of the cup, we can concentrate on the league,' said Ryan during a lunchtime soccer practice. 'At least we can still win that.'

'Dead right,' grunted Pud. 'League's more important, in any case. Proves who's the best team over the whole season.'

Pud was fit again. Or as fit as he was ever going to be. He carried too much

bulk around his middle to have a chance of outrunning anybody. He didn't need to. He tripped them up instead before they could run away.

'We missed you against Shenby,' said Ryan.

Pud beamed, flattered by the compliment, until Jamie piped up.

'Yeah, you being away sure left a big hole in the team!'

'Watch it, Gingernut,' Pud growled, assuming Jamie was trying to be cheeky as usual. They enjoyed trading insults with each other.

Mr Jones interrupted the banter. 'Come on, let's see some action there. I want you three to sharpen up your shooting boots for Saturday.'

Danebridge had another league match to play at home first before they renewed their battle with Shenby. As the visitors were bottom of the table, the boys saw it as a golden opportunity to boost their goal tally.

Especially Pud. His cannonball shooting was a threat to the health and safety of any goalkeeper.

'I'm gonna fill my boots against Eastgate,' he boasted.

Jamie grinned. 'Reckon you fill them pretty good already. Your feet are massive.'

'What I mean, Clever Dick, is that I'm gonna score ten goals.'

'About the only time you'll ever count to ten!'

Pud was riled and suddenly lashed a ball goalwards. Chris wasn't even ready and it was only his quick reflexes that saved him from decapitation. He saw the ball at the last moment and ducked his head out of the way a split second before he might have had it knocked off.

He gave Pud a hard stare. 'No need to guess who hit that one. Go back a bit, will you. You're too close.'

The three strikers kept Chris busy during the shooting practice. They looked on good form, and so did Chris, but he was grateful they were using small-sized goals.

It took a very good shot indeed to beat him and Pud produced it. He

connected with a short pass from Ryan so sweetly that the ball seemed to gather pace as it flashed through the air and into the net. It barely rose off the ground, leaving Chris flailing in its slipstream.

'Almost broke the land speed record there, Big Fellow,' Jamie praised him to get back into Pud's good books for a while.

At the end of the session, Mr Jones named the team to play Eastgate. 'Don't take it for granted that you'll have an easy win,' he warned them. 'Anything can happen in football. It's a funny old game, as they say.'

He didn't hear Philip muttering at the back of the group.

'Huh! They wouldn't have said that if they'd come up against Wally. There isn't much to laugh about when *he's* blowing his whistle.'

the back of the group.
'Huh! They wouldn't have said that
if they'd come up against Wally. There
isn't much to laugh about when he's

# 4 Put to the Test

Next morning, the footballers of
Danebridge did not find the start of
their game at all amusing. Eastgate
opened the scoring in the very first
minute. Or at least that's what the
referee decided.

Chris took the sting out of a fierce
shot but was helpless to prevent the
ball rolling towards the net. To his
relief, Jordan managed to scramble
back in time, stretch out a foot and
hook the ball away.

'Thanks, great covering,' cried Chris as the visitors claimed a goal.

'That was in, ref,' came a shout from the touchline.

'Ball went over the line,' insisted their number eight. 'I saw it.'

Mr Jones, the referee, hesitated a moment and then made up his mind. He pointed to the centre-circle and the Eastgate team danced away in celebration. His own players were left

gaping. No-one actually dared to say anything, but he guessed what they were thinking.

'Hard to tell whether or not the whole ball had crossed the line before Jordan got a boot to it,' Mr Jones explained, half apologetically. 'I had to give Eastgate the benefit of the doubt. That's only fair.'

'*Fair*, he says!' Philip snorted as soon as the headmaster was out of earshot. 'After what happened to us last Saturday!'

'That's probably why he favoured them,' sighed Chris. 'Nothing we can do about it now apart from try and equalize.'

That was easier said than done. For a while, it seemed to be one of those days when the ball simply refused to go in the net. Danebridge were dominating the game, but chance after chance went begging. Pud miskicked in front of an open goal, Ryan fired another sitter over the bar and Jamie dribbled himself dizzy in ever-decreasing circles.

And when they did get any shots on target, the ball flew straight into the Eastgate goalkeeper's gloves like a well-trained homing pigeon.

Only as the seconds ticked away towards the break did Danebridge finally succeed. Even then, they needed a helping hand – or head. Ryan floated in a harmless-looking cross into the goalmouth and a defender panicked. He heard the pounding of heavy feet behind him and headed the

ball under the bar instead of over it as he tried to clear.

'The kid had to play the ball,' said Pud during the half-time team-talk. 'He knew I was right behind him if he left it.'

'I bet he did,' grinned Jamie. 'He must have thought he was going to get flattened by a runaway elephant!'

It was a good job for Jamie that Pud was in a better mood after the embarrassment of his earlier miss. And that Mr Jones stood between them.

'It's just a matter of time now,' said the headmaster. 'Be patient. Keep playing the way you are, making chances, and the goals will come.'

He was right. Chris hardly had a touch of the ball in the second half as Danebridge clicked into top gear. He was as much of a spectator as Grandad who was standing on the touchline with Shoot, their border collie.

Chris enjoyed the dog's reactions every time a goal was scored. Shoot joined in with the antics of the excited people around them, jumping up at Grandad and barking madly, not sure what all the fuss was about. He preferred chasing cats and sticks to watching football matches.

After Jamie put Danebridge ahead from Ryan's pass, the goalie's pigeons must have fled the loft. The two wingers ran riot, scoring two goals each, before Jamie set Pud up for the sixth and final strike.

Jamie saw Pud in space outside the penalty area and surprised everyone by passing the ball to him. 'All yours, Big Fellow,' he called out.

Pud was desperate to add his own name to the scoresheet that Mr Jones always put on the sports noticeboard after a game. He hammered the ball with all his might and the goalie made sure he wasn't in the way of the thunderbolt. He didn't want to go

home himself with dislocated fingers.

'Six of the best!' cried Philip. 'Watch out, Wally, here we come!'

On the following Friday, at morning break, Chris called a private team meeting in a sheltered corner of the windy playground.

'If we want to be champions this season, we can't afford to lose to Shenby again,' he stressed, 'but . . .'

He was immediately interrupted. 'Right, but we're playing against twelve men,' said Philip. 'Them and their ref.'

'Yeah, looks like we'll have to make them use a sub,' Pud smirked. 'If I collided with Wally, sort of accidentally on purpose, he might have to be carried off. Jonesy could take over then.'

'He'd probably give them more goals

than Wally,' Jordan scoffed.

Chris brought the meeting to order. 'Look, I've said we need to win, but it's got to be done in the right way. If we let Wally rattle us, we've had it. We've got to keep our heads and play it cool.'

The captain could see that some of the team were not yet convinced and he wanted to make sure his message was taken seriously.

'Jonesy very nearly called this match off, you know, but I reckon he's testing us instead,' Chris continued. 'If we show any dissent to Wally, he might even stop the game and hand the points to Shenby. Just imagine how we'd feel then.'

'So what are we gonna do?' said Jordan. 'Let them walk all over us?'

'No way!' Pud muttered. 'Nobody walks over me.'

'Quicker than trying to walk round you,' Jamie quipped.

Chris put a restraining hand on Pud's arm as the striker made a move towards the joker.

'We've *all* got to pass Jonesy's test –

including you, Pud. One flash of your temper against the ref and we could be on our way home early. And that could be the last time you'll ever play for the school . . .'

Chris confessed his worries about the game to Andrew when he got home that afternoon. 'Are you still thinking of coming with us to watch?'

'No – I'll already be there.' Andrew grinned at his brother's puzzled face. 'Didn't I tell you? I'm staying over at Gaz's place tonight. Nice and handy then for the big match in the morning.'

'Look, I don't really care if you're there or not, but please don't do anything to show us up, OK?'

'As if I would,' Andrew said, the picture of innocence. 'We're just gonna fix a few things with Dominic for tomorrow, that's all.'

'What d'yer mean by that?' Chris

said gruffly. 'Stay out of it, will you. We had enough fixing going on last time.'

'Relax, our kid, no need to lose any sleep over it,' Andrew chuckled. 'Well, can't stand here chatting all day. Must pack my bag. Got places to go, people to see . . .'

Chris feared the worst. He was in for a restless night.

# 5 Nightmare Game

Chris stared at the football in dismay.
It sat in the back of the net, mocking
him as he lay in a pool of muddy water.
Beaten yet again.

He'd lost count of the score. It must
have been about 10–0 to Shenby. He
reckoned half the goals were offside,
two should have been ruled out for
handball and Chris had saved another
of them before it crossed the line. But
Wally awarded a goal every single
time.

Now Matthew had just scored from a penalty for a foul by Philip outside the area. And to make matters even worse, Wally had gone and sent Philip off. He'd already given Pud his marching orders.

Chris staggered to his feet and glanced towards Grandad to seek some advice about what to do. He could hardly believe his eyes. Grandad was invading the pitch, waving his fists at the referee.

Nobody else seemed to have noticed. Pud was too busy kicking Matthew until his victim sank to his knees and cried out for mercy.

Chris tried to cut Grandad off, but his legs felt like lead weights. He wasn't able to get there in time. Then Andrew rode on to the pitch on his bike. He reached the referee first and punched the teacher himself. Wally toppled to the ground, blood pouring from his nose.

The whole playing field had become a chaotic free-for-all. Fights had broken out between the two sets of players and among the parents on the touchline. Even Shoot was involved, barking and snarling at people. Chris couldn't understand why Mr Jones was doing nothing to stop it. He was just standing in the centre-circle and laughing.

Chris screamed and then put his fingers into his mouth to give a loud whistle, hoping it would make everybody come to their senses . . .

He woke up in a cold sweat. It was still dark. He didn't know where he was until a door opened and let in a stream of light. A dog also bounded in and began licking at his face.

'What on earth is all that noise about?' asked Mum, pulling Shoot away. 'Are you all right? You've been screaming and whistling.'

Chris looked around the bedroom in a daze, still trying to gather his wits. It had all seemed so very real.

'Sorry, Mum,' he said lamely. 'Must have been having a bad dream.'

'I'll say it was. You've kicked all your bedclothes on to the floor and it looks like you've been fighting with your pillow.'

Chris gazed at the devastated bed and grinned. 'Just practising for the match. We're gonna sort Shenby out.'

'Well, you can sort your bed out first,' she said. 'At least you haven't gone and wet it!'

'Aw, Mum!' he said in disgust. 'You know I never do that. A good goalie always keeps clean sheets!'

\*

Chris emerged from the Shenby school cloakroom to spot Andrew against the fence on the far side of the pitch. Gaz

and Dominic were there too, surrounded by a bunch of blue shirts. The discussions looked to be pretty lively with lots of arm-waving.

'Wonder what that's all about?' he mused, suspiciously.

As Chris went across to investigate, the group broke up and most of the Shenby players drifted away. A white-faced Matthew was among them.

'Hiya, little brother,' Andrew greeted him cheerily. 'Bet you missed me last night. Sleep well?'

'Not exactly,' Chris muttered. 'Had things on my mind.'

'Told you, Gaz. Always a worrier, our kid. That's why I have to help him out at times.'

'I can do without your kind of help,' said Chris, thinking of his night-marish battlefield. He was glad Andrew didn't have his bike with him.

'Huh! That's all the thanks we get for trying to do him a favour.'

'Typical!' Gaz joined in. 'We'll see if he changes his tune later on.'

They sauntered off, sniggering,

leaving the two captains staring at each other awkwardly.

'Something's going on, isn't it?' said Chris. 'What's the big secret?'

'Nothing,' Dominic replied, glancing round nervously. 'Well, nothing I can let on about right now. You'll find out soon enough when it happens . . . *if* it happens.'

'If *what* happens?' persisted Chris, anxious to get to the bottom of the mystery. 'Are our brothers behind all this?'

'No, it's a kind of team effort, really – but it was you who first put the idea into my head after the cup match.'

Chris was stunned. 'Me? How?'

'Soz, got to go and speak to someone,' said Dominic, avoiding the questions. He ran off to catch Matthew up and Chris saw him take the number seven to one side for a private talk.

The Danebridge captain gave a shrug and went to inspect the pitch, which was soggy and slippery after the overnight rain. When he reached one of the goalmouths, he suddenly realized there were no nets on the posts. Nor on those at the other end. His teammates had already noticed.

'Gives Wally a better chance of pulling a fast one,' growled Philip.

'How d'yer mean?' asked Ryan. 'It's the same for both sides.'

'Not with Wally as ref, it isn't. He's up to something, I bet.'

'He's not the only one either,' Chris murmured under his breath.

The match began ominously for Danebridge. Pud was penalized twice in the opening minutes, once for pushing and then for scoring. He beat the Shenby goalkeeper with a powerful drive from the edge of the penalty area, but his delight quickly gave way to amazement.

'No goal!' announced the referee. 'Offside.'

'I wasn't offside,' Pud protested.

Mr Walters glared at him. 'Your number eleven was in an offside position when you shot.'

'He wasn't interfering with play.'

'Don't argue with me, lad. I've made a decision. No goal.'

While the goalkeeper fetched the ball, Pud stood fuming in frustration, hands on hips. Steam almost seemed to be coming out of his ears.

'Sorry, Big Fellow,' said Jamie. 'Must have strayed too far forward.'

'Not your fault – for once,' Pud muttered. 'That cheat was just using you as an excuse.'

'Not sure I like the look of this,' remarked Grandad. 'Things might get a bit out of hand here soon.'

Mr Jones nodded. 'I'm beginning to wish that I'd followed my better judgement and cancelled this game.'

'Too late now, I'm afraid. We'll just have to keep our fingers crossed and hope for the best.'

Luck was certainly with Danebridge a minute later when they enjoyed a let-off themselves. Matthew swivelled and hit a snapshot on the turn beyond Chris's reach, but the ball smacked against the top of the post and rebounded back into play.

'Surprised the ref didn't say the ball crossed the line,' said Jordan sarcastically after Philip cleared the danger. 'Especially as it was his precious son.'

'Give him time. Don't touch Matthew inside the area whatever you do. Even shaking his hand would earn them a penalty.'

'How about shaking him by the throat?'

Philip grinned. 'Only when the ref's not looking.'

Shenby were a good enough side in their own right not to need any extra help from the referee. He was determined, however, to give it to them. The favouritism he showed was so blatant that even the Shenby parents began to laugh at his bizarre decisions in order to hide their embarrassment. The Danebridge supporters felt more like crying.

It came as a total shock to everyone, therefore, when Danebridge broke away to score and the goal was allowed to stand.

# 6 *Like Father, Like Son?*

The Shenby goalkeeper hung his head in shame.

Jamie's hopeful cross from the left wing had plopped straight into his arms – and out again. The wet ball was like a bar of soap in the bath, and he'd let it slip out of his grasp and over the line.

As a former goalie, Grandad couldn't help feeling a little sorry for the boy. 'I think he was wise not to try and catch

the ref's eye,' he chuckled to himself.
'Just in case he went and dropped that
too!'

Inside two minutes, however, the
goalkeeper's mistake was cancelled
out by Matthew's volley. But the only
person who saw it as an equalizing
goal was the one in charge – the
referee.

Chris had the shot well covered, diving to make sure the ball couldn't squeeze between him and the post. He was horrified when he realized the referee had given a goal. Even Matthew looked astonished by the decision and turned away, showing no pleasure in scoring. He knew he hadn't.

'That went wide!' Chris protested. 'Would have hit the side netting.'

'Not from my angle,' said Mr Walters. 'The goal stands. One–all.'

A loud cry rang out over the playing field. 'What a wally! You're not even any good at cheating, ref!'

The furious referee scanned the touchline for the culprit, without success. Chris knew who it was of course. He picked out Andrew peering from behind the shelter of a tree.

At half-time, the Danebridge players were still angry at the injustice of the goal and had never seen their headmaster so upset.

'Bet Jonesy won't say anything today about the ref always being right!' muttered Philip.

Their attention was caught by raised voices from the Shenby group some distance away. A few of the boys' parents seemed to be making their feelings known to Mr Walters very strongly.

'He's got a revolt on his hands, by the look of it,' said Mr Jones. 'Deserves it too, the way he's been acting.'

'I always said that Shenby were revolting,' grinned Pud.

'C'mon, team,' Chris rallied them as they took up their positions for the delayed second half. 'They're bound to be a bit shaken up for a while after all that arguing. Let's get at 'em. We can still win this game.'

They did their best to follow the captain's instructions. Both Jamie and Ryan had shots on target, but each time the keeper was equal to the task. He was careful to position his body right behind the line of the ball and the two saves helped to restore his confidence.

To their credit, Shenby settled down and hit back, giving as good as they got. A firm header brought Chris into action, too, alert as ever to any danger. He was grateful, though, to see a powerful, swirling shot clip

Philip on the shoulder and deflect safely over the crossbar.

'Handball! Penalty kick,' announced the referee, to the disbelief of everybody, on and off the pitch. 'You take it, Matthew.'

'But it was nowhere near his hand, Dad.'

'Don't *you* start now. Just do as you're told, lad.'

There were boos coming from the touchline, and not just from Andrew and other Danebridge supporters. Many of the Shenby people were joining in too.

Matthew was visibly trembling as he placed the ball on the penalty spot. He turned and glanced at Dominic on the edge of the area in a silent, desperate appeal for help. The captain sensed that his teammate might not have the nerve to carry out the agreed plan.

Gaz doubted it too. He made a strange sight by the corner flag. He was frantically waving his brother forward, miming a kick at an imaginary ball.

As Matthew took several steps back and the whistle sounded, Dominic suddenly brushed past him. Chris was taken by surprise but didn't need to bother diving. Dominic scooped the ball almost comically high over the bar, as if he'd done it on purpose.

The cheers and laughter died away as the referee insisted the penalty be retaken. 'Doesn't count. You can't switch kickers at the last moment like that,' he declared, bending the rules to his own advantage.

'I don't mind – he missed,' said Chris. 'It should be a goal-kick.'

Mr Walters ignored him and grabbed Dominic by the arm. 'I don't know what you think you're playing at,' he hissed. 'I'll deal with you later.'

Dominic shrugged, pulled himself free and gave Matthew a little nod of encouragement as they passed each other. 'Go on, Matt, you can do it,' the captain urged. 'Show him how we all feel.'

Matthew replaced the ball and looked up at Chris. 'Just stay where you are,' he said, forcing a sickly grin.

Chris was confused. He thought Matthew must be trying to taunt him, but the boy looked in no mood for playing any tricks.

Matthew moved in, but slowed as he neared the ball and simply tapped it along the ground straight at the keeper. The ball barely reached him. All Chris had to do was bend down and pick it up.

Mr Walters stared open-mouthed at his son.

'Sorry, Dad, I just didn't think it was fair to score . . .'

Matthew dried up, his face deathly pale as he waited for his father to erupt. But the explosion never came.

The spark had gone out.

The rest of the Shenby team gathered around to support Matthew and Dominic. The captain gulped, took a deep breath, and then spoke up. He'd been rehearsing what to say with Gaz and Andrew.

'We want to win as much as anybody, Mr Walters, but not at all costs. It's not right. We don't like people thinking we're cheats.'

The teacher nodded dumbly, not knowing how to respond. Then he turned on his heel, trudged across to Mr Jones and offered him the whistle.

'Sorry I've been such a fool. I realize that now, thanks to these lads, and I feel ashamed of myself. Please take over from me.'

The headmaster shook his head. 'I'm hardly dressed for the part,' he smiled, pointing at his wellies. 'You carry on. It won't do any harm for the boys to see that teachers can learn their lessons too.'

Mr Walters, duly humbled, repeated his apologies to the players. 'I'll award you the game, if you like,' he said to the

Danebridge team. 'It might make up a little for the cup match.'

'No need for that,' Chris replied. 'Like Dominic, all we want is a fair contest – win, lose or draw.'

'Right, so let's get this ball rolling again,' said the referee. 'Score's still one–all – and may the best team win.'

The game was played in a strange atmosphere for the next few minutes as the footballers tried to pick up the momentum. For the Shenby boys, it felt almost like an anti-climax after the success of their revolution.

Dominic brought the match back to life when he tested Chris's reflexes from close-range. The opposing captain blocked the shot and dived on the rebound before Dominic could follow it up.

'This is more like it, eh?' said Dominic, helping Chris to his feet.

'Yeah, better late than never,' he grinned.

Both goalies were kept busy for the remaining minutes of the game. Shenby's had his hands warmed by Jordan's rocket and also held on to a looping header from Philip that was destined for the top corner.

Matthew had been understandably subdued since the penalty incident, but perked up when given the chance to run with the ball. He almost twisted Jordan inside-out with a skilful dribble down the wing, creating space for a shot that Chris only smothered at the second attempt.

'Well played, son, great effort,' his dad praised him. 'And well saved, too, keeper.'

What finally convinced Danebridge that the referee had turned over a new leaf was when he blew for offside

against Shenby in the next attack. It was their first free-kick in either game.

And they made it count. It was from Jordan's quick pass to Jamie that Danebridge regained the lead.

Jamie cantered away with the ball up the left wing, riding a couple of challenges like a jockey in a steeplechase race. The going was very soft. He squelched through a large puddle, losing control for a moment, but just managed to squirt the ball across to Pud.

Danebridge's carthorse did the rest. Pud's pent-up feelings were all released in his ferocious whack at the ball. It was one of his special master-blasters. The poor goalkeeper had a long trek to retrieve the ball.

The goal made the score 2–1 and proved to be the winning strike. Mr

Walters didn't dare allow much added time in case Shenby grabbed an equalizer. He didn't want to be accused of playing on until they scored.

Everyone was glad to hear the final whistle and put the match behind them. Chris even went up to shake the referee's hand this time before seeking out Dominic. The two captains were joined in the centre-circle by their older brothers.

'Nice one, Dom!' cried Gaz. 'You did it, kid. Knew you could stand up to that Wally.'

Andrew slapped Dominic on the back. 'The plan worked like a dream.'

'What plan was that exactly?' asked Chris.

'Well, we guessed Wally would give us a penalty we didn't deserve,' explained Dominic. 'We decided that was the best time to have a kind of showdown with him. We should have done it before, like you said.'

'What about Matthew? Bet he took a bit of persuading.'

'Yeah, he did, but it all worked out well in the end.'

'Apart from the fact that you lost,' put in Gaz.

'It was worth it. We've made our point.'

'Looks like all is forgiven, anyway,' said Chris, nodding towards the school. The teacher was walking alongside Matthew, his arm around his son's shoulders. 'Wally ought to be grateful for what you did today.'

'Why's that?'

'For reminding him that cheats never prosper!'

**THE END**

# ABOUT THE AUTHOR

Rob Childs was born and grew up in Derby. His childhood ambition was to become an England cricketer or footballer – preferably both! After university, however, he went into teaching and taught in primary and high schools in Leicestershire, where he now lives. Always interested in school sports, he coached school teams and clubs across a range of sports, and ran area representative teams in football, cricket and athletics.

Recognizing a need for sports fiction for young readers, he decided to have a go at writing such stories himself and now has more than fifty books to his name, including the popular *The Big Match* series, published by Young Corgi Books.

Rob has now left teaching in order to be able to write full-time. Married to Joy, also a writer, Rob has a 'lassie' dog called Laddie and is also a keen photographer.

# THE BIG FREEZE
## *by Rob Childs*

*'Bottom of the table!' moaned Pud.
'We've no chance of qualifying for
the Final now.'*

The big freeze is wrecking the team's
soccer season – they haven't played a
proper match for two months and
the novelty of playing indoors has
long worn off.

But then Jamie's father books them in
for sessions on the all-weather pitches
at the new sport centre, and they find
themselves taking part in an exciting
triangular tournament. But will Pud be
able to keep his feet on the unfamiliar
surface? And will the big-headed Carl
Diamond keep them out of the Final?

ISBN 0 552 52967 2

Available in all good book stores

YOUNG CORGI BOOKS